MW00743852

The DREAM BIG Academy
rosie wants to be a fireman

To my Princess Sienna Briele:
When I grow up, I want to be just like you.
I love you. Dream Big!

xoxo

Always, Mommy

Published by rissylyn

Printed in the United States of America

First Edition: June 2013

Print Edition ISBN 978-0-9894933-0-7

Illustrations by Brooke Hagel: http://fabulousdoodles.blogspot.com/

Visit Dreambigacademy.com for more information

The DREAM BIG Academy
rosie wants to be a fireman

by Marissa Klein

ILLUSTRATED BY BROOKE HAGEL

Yea! I hear a key in the door. I jump to my feet and skip across the floor. You're home! You came back! I missed you all day! Come to my room so we can all play!

It's Daddy's turn to make me laugh. It's Mommy's turn to run my bath.

"What did you do today and where did you play? Tell us what made this a wonderful day."

I took a deep breath. Just where should I start? Do I talk about school or what I made in art?

Oh, I know! I know! I saw that truck with the noise. It was big. It was red and looked like one of my toys. "Hmmm," Mommy said, "what could it be?" Daddy said, "a fire truck, Rosie, it sounds like to me!"

Off to the potty and teeth time we go. PJs and nightlights, it's the bedtime show! We sing our goodnight song and turn on the machine that makes sound. Daddy flies me into bed, with kisses all around.

"Sweet dreams, Princess Rosie. Can we sleep in your cribby?" No Mommy, no Daddy, you both are too biggie! I lie down with Ellie and just like we said, I fall fast asleep with big dreams in my head.

Ellie and I were drawing with chalk, when we heard the sirens from down the sidewalk. The noise was loud as it came near and soon there was a fireman talking right in my ear.

"Hello, Rosie, I need you to help me. Jump in the front and bring little Ellie." All of a sudden, the Chief said, "See, there's a kitty-cat up in your tree." Oh no! It's Piper! How did he get up there? How can we get him? We can't sit and stare!

The fireman pointed to the back of his truck. There sat a black and white doggie whose name was Chuck! "Woof, woof," barked Chuck, "we brought some milk and a cup. Let's show it to Piper, so he'll come lick it up."

The Chief pushed a button and we started to climb, Chuck with me, and Ellie close behind. Here Piper, here, come take a lick. It's safe on the ladder. We'll rescue you quick.

Slowly but surely, Piper stepped toward us. He jumped in my arms without any fuss. Chuck carried us down on his long waggy tail and the Chief shut off the siren's loud wail.

Our neighbors were cheering at Piper smiling so wide. Oh you silly cat, don't go up trees to hide!

The Chief took out his bullhorn and shouted, "Yippee! Chuck, Ellie, and Rosie, you set Piper free! What helpers and heroes you turned out to be. Today we'll make you firemen trainees!"

But Chief, I want to be a real fireman now and Ellie does too. How can we drive the truck and rescue like you? "Oh Rosie," says Chief, "you've got plenty of time, to be a good girl and continue to shine. When you grow up you can be whatever you dream. The world is yours to chase," he winked with a gleam.

"But now it's time to go back to your bed and rest on your pillow your pretty head. Dream big, Princess Rosie, and Ellie in tow, dream big every night and day that you grow!"

Thank you, Chief, and bye-bye, Chuck! What a fun ride on your fire truck. Shh, Ellie, let's lie down and close our eyes. Soon Mommy and Daddy will be singing the sunrise.

"You are my sunshine, my only sunshine," my Mommy did call. I see that it's morning so soon, after all. Morning Mommy! Guess what I want to be? "What my darling? Tell us, Sweet Pea."

I want to be a fireman just like the Chief, and Chuck. Ellie and I will help kitties get unstuck. Did you hear the sirens as they pulled away from our house? Piper was so happy when he hugged his stuffed mouse!

"What sirens? What Chief?" Daddy asked. "Who is this Chuck?" Oh, Mommy and Daddy, we rode in the truck! We climbed up the ladder and had such a night. We dreamed we were firemen. We dreamed big, all right.

"What a nice story, tell us more while you eat. It's time to start our day and we got you a treat." Mommy said, "Close your green eyes," and Daddy said, "1, 2, 3, surprise!"

My very own fire hat! Wow! Ellie, look at me! Just like the Chief in our dream last night, see? Daddy, can I be a fireman for real some day?

"Of course you can, Princess, just like we always say, every night when you dream, you to get to be whatever you want.

Today it's a fireman; tomorrow, who knows? But your mind fills with wonder, as you sleep and you grow!"

I can't wait for tonight and when you get back. We'll all play firemen with me in my hat! We will climb up ladders and rescue a cat.

"We'll tell funny stories while you're in the tub, but until then, give us a hug. We're so excited you learned to be a fireman, in the school of your dreams. It's your very own Dream Academy, or so it seems!"

With love and gratitude to my favorite dreamers:

My Choice family—we have been putting people to work since 1974! And the stories we can tell...

My Soul family—you raised the bar on chasing dreams! Especially Lindsay , Kara, Kathy, Laurie, Julie and Elizabeth—and you each know your "why."

My Mommy & Daddy & baby sister, Jamie! Thank you for...well, all of it (including Books Galore) SAFE.

Courtney & Chicago—I wrote this book while waiting for a plane at O'Hare—what a great visit!

To my partner in crime, David—for accusing me of being a Dreamer on 21st and 9th in 2003. I have been busy living up to that title ever since. Thank you for the balance.

And to my Sienna & Summer—You are my sunshines. Thank you for the lightening speed molasses and for filling my life with joy.

ABOUT THE AUTHOR

Marissa Klein knows a little something about dreaming big. After building her career in beauty and fashion sales in NYC, she finally embraced her inner entrepreneur, left the corporate world behind, and started a successful handmade and custom gift company, Rissy Lyn. Throughout her travels, Marissa was always the "matchmaker"—constantly connecting people, helping people, talking to people, changing people. So, while promoting her namesake brand at one of the many trunk shows at Henri Bendel, she had an epiphany: why not bring these skills together and help others dream the way she always had? For the past 8 years, she has managed Choice Fashion/Media, the creative division of her family's boutique staffing firm. Everyday, she helps people find their dream jobs. She believes that while inherently we may have more "grown-up" realities, at the end of the day, we all just want to be able to do what we love and be genuinely happy doing it. Marissa is originally from Harrington Park, NJ, and graduated from the University of Richmond with a degree in business. She currently resides in Hoboken, NJ, with her husband David, her two beautiful dreamers, Sienna and Summer, and her poodle, Simba.

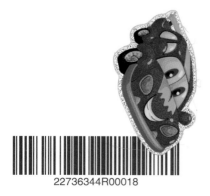

Made in the USA
Charleston, SC
30 September 2013